This book should be returned to any branch of the
Lancashire County Library on or before the date shown

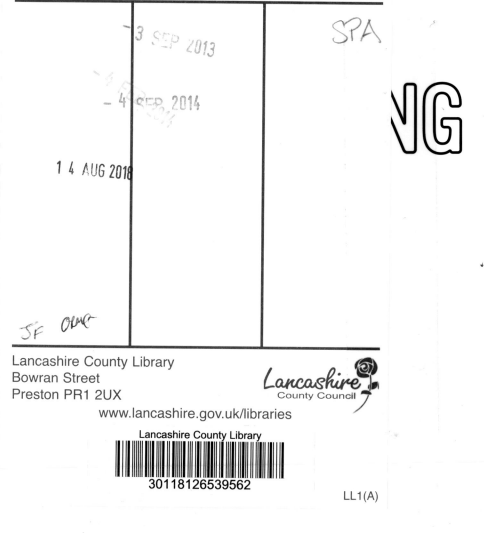

Lancashire County Library
Bowran Street
Preston PR1 2UX

Lancashire
County Council

www.lancashire.gov.uk/libraries

LL1(A)

TITLES AT THIS LEVEL

Fiction

978 1 4451 1812 3 pb

978 1 4451 1811 6 pb

978 1 4451 1813 0 pb

Graphic fiction

978 1 4451 1799 7 pb

978 1 4451 1801 7 pb

978 1 4451 1800 0 pb

Non-fiction

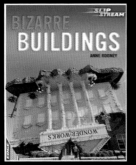

978 1 4451 1952 6

978 1 4451 1954 0

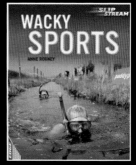

978 1 4451 1953 3

VAMPIRES ARE SO BORING

DAVID AND HELEN ORME
Illustrated by PAUL DAVIDSON

EDGE
FRANKLIN WATTS

LONDON • SYDNEY

First published in 2013 by
Franklin Watts
338 Euston Road
London NW1 3BH

Franklin Watts Australia
Level 17/207 Kent Street
Sydney NSW 2000

Text © David and Helen Orme 2013
Illustration © Franklin Watts 2013

The rights of David and Helen Orme to be
identified as the authors and Paul Davidson
as the illustrator of this Work have been
asserted in accordance with the Copyright,
Designs and Patents Act, 1988.

A CIP catalogue record for this book is
available from the British Library.

ISBN 978 1 4451 1813 0

Series Editors: Adrian Cole and Jackie Hamley
Series Advisors: Diana Bentley and Dee Reid
Series Designer: Peter Scoulding

1 3 5 7 9 10 8 6 4 2

Printed in China

Franklin Watts is a division of
Hachette Children's Books,
an Hachette UK company.
www.hachette.co.uk

CONTENTS

CHAPTER 1
THE VAMPIRE WAKES

In the churchyard, the stone cross

on a tomb shook. Then it fell over.

Slowly, the lid of the tomb slid open.

A thin mist crept out.

The mist swirled and formed into a boy.

"Blood! I must have blood!" he whispered.

After so many years in the tomb he was

weak. A rat ran over his foot.

"My first taste of blood for a long time,"

thought the vampire.

The blood made him stronger. Now he

could hunt for real food — human blood!

He waited in the shadows.

CHAPTER 2
SCREAMING GIRLS

Two girls were walking across the churchyard.

When they saw him, one of the girls screamed.

But they did not run away. Instead they ran

towards him.

"No way — it's a real vampire!" shouted

one girl.

She put her arms round him and tried to

kiss him.

"Why aren't you scared?" cried the vampire.

They were both still screaming at him.

After a thousand years of silence the vampire

could not stand the noise.

"It's just like that show on the telly,"

said one girl. "You can be my boyfriend."

"You can give up being a vampire," said the other. "We'll help you, don't be afraid!"

He backed off, but they grabbed hold of him.

"Come with us," they said. "We'll show you what life is like now."

CHAPTER 3
VAMPIRE DATE

The girls dragged the vampire away from the churchyard. Away from the dark. It was horrible. There were lights everywhere and so much noise.

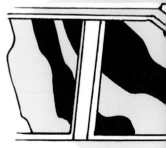

They took him to a clothes shop.

"You need to dress a bit better if you want

to hang out with us!" said one girl.

"Try these on!" cried the other girl.

Then they took him to a nightclub. It was even

louder than the street. The vampire couldn't

stand the noise. And the girls' mates all

wanted to have their photos taken with him.

CHAPTER 4
CAN I GO NOW?

"Take me back," begged the vampire. "I'll go back to my tomb. Just make sure the cross is put back to keep me safe."

The girls led him back to the graveyard.

The vampire misted back into his tomb.

The girls looked at each other.

"Vampires are SO boring!" they agreed.

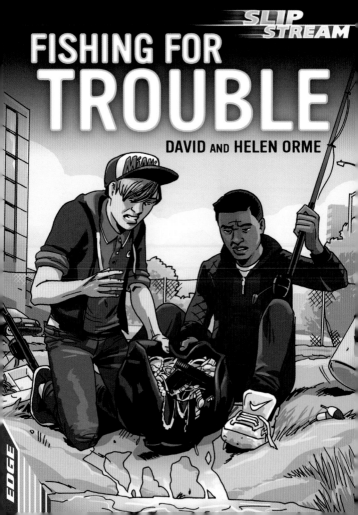

Will and Adam go fishing every weekend.
It keeps them away from the gangs on their estate.

Then, one day, they catch more
than they bargained for.

How will they keep out of trouble now?

EDGE
FRANKLIN
WATTS

LONDON•SYDNEY

FOOTBALL
LEGEND

DAVID AND HELEN ORME

EDGE

Rob is always being picked on by Martin.
This time, it's for hanging out with his granddad.

But with the school football trials looming, perhaps
hanging out with Granddad isn't such a bad idea...

EDGE
FRANKLIN
WATTS

LONDON•SYDNEY

About

SLIP STREAM

Slipstream is a series of expertly levelled books designed for pupils who are struggling with reading. Its unique three-strand approach through fiction, graphic fiction and non-fiction gives pupils a rich reading experience that will accelerate their progress and close the reading gap.

At the heart of every Slipstream fiction book is a great story. Easily accessible words and phrases ensure that pupils both decode and comprehend, and the high interest stories really engage older struggling readers.

Whether you're using Slipstream Level 2 for Guided Reading or as an independent read, here are some suggestions:

1. Make each reading session successful. Talk about the text before the pupil starts reading. Introduce any unfamiliar vocabulary.

2. Encourage the pupil to talk about the book using a range of open questions. For example, who would they most like to meet?

3. Discuss the differences between reading fiction, graphic fiction and non-fiction. What do they prefer?

Slipstream Level 2 photocopiable **WORKBOOK** ISBN: 978 1 4451 1797 3 available – download free sample worksheets from: www.franklinwatts.co.uk

For guidance, SLIPSTREAM Level 2 – Vampires Are So Boring has been approximately measured to:

National Curriculum Level: 2b
Reading Age: 7.6–8.0
Book Band: Purple

ATOS: 2.4*
Guided Reading Level: I
Lexile® Measure (confirmed): 380L

*Please check actual Accelerated Reader™ book level and quiz availability at www.arbookfind.co.uk